WHISPERS IN THE WIRE

BY ASH BLACKWOOD

DEDICATION PAGE

For the dreamers, the fighters, and the ones who rise again. For those who have stood in the ashes of yesterday and still dared to face tomorrow's dawn. This is for you the unbroken, the reborn, the eternal flame.

ACKNOWLEDGMENTS

This book rose from more than my own fire — it carries the sparks of many hearts and hands. To my family, who believed in me when the embers were faint, thank you for fanning the flames of my dream. To my friends and mentors, whose guidance and encouragement kept me steady through the storms, you are the wind beneath these phoenix wings.

To my readers, who choose to journey with me into worlds of fire, ash, and rebirth, your belief fuels every word I write. And to every soul who has ever felt consumed by the flames, may you find your way through the smoke and rise again.

AUTHOR'S NOTE

There is a moment in every journey when the fire seems too fierce, when the smoke blinds you, and the way forward feels impossible. From the Ashes was born from that place. It is a story of burning away the false, the broken, and the lost — and finding in the embers a truth worth rising for.

My hope is that within these pages, you'll find your own spark — the one that will carry you through the darkness, no matter how deep it feels.

Rise. Always rise.

Whispers In The Wire – Legal & Copyright Page Draft

First Edition

Cover design by Ash Blackwood

Interior design by Ash Blackwood

Printed in the United States

Table of content

Chapter One

The Incident

The Baltimore heat was oppressive an invisible force that sat on Marcus Caldwell's shoulders and wrapped around his chest like a vice. The sun beat down from a merciless sky, bleaching the cracked pavement of Liberty Heights into a glaring, white-hot haze. Cicadas buzzed from the trees, their shrill symphony rising and falling like some cosmic warning. It was the kind of heat that made tempers short, made patience an endangered species. It made people forget themselves.

Marcus sat in the passenger seat of his father's aging Crown Vic, his legs sticking to the cracked faux leather, his T-shirt soaked down the back. The AC had long since given up, a casualty of years and disrepair.

The vents exhaled little more than the ghost of cool air, useless against the furnace outside. But the car ran, a testament to James Caldwell's stubborn will, and in this part of town, that was what mattered.

He cracked the window, hoping for a breeze, but the air outside was no better. Just hot, thick, like breathing through cotton. Still, he didn't complain. Not out loud. Not today. Today was different. Today, they were trying. His father, Detective James Caldwell, was trying.

He'd picked Marcus up that morning with a hopeful glint in his eye and a pat on the back that landed too hard, like he was trying to communicate something he couldn't quite say. That was his way broad gestures and narrow silences. Marcus hadn't seen him much in the last few months. Between his mom's simmering bitterness and James's unpredictable schedule, they were like two planets in orbit, always missing each other by a few hours, a few essential moments.

James Caldwell hadn't always kept an apartment downtown near the precinct, half-furnished and mostly empty a place to crash after late shifts or stakeouts that bled into sunrise. His hours were brutal, his phone constantly buzzing with the urgent rhythm of the streets.

He chased leads like a man possessed, trying to clean the city's veins while holding together a marriage fraying at the seams. Veronica had begged him to come home. Not just physically but emotionally. For Marcus. For her. Eventually, he did. He moved back into their rowhouse in West Baltimore, the air thick with unspoken apologies and years of neglect. But by then, the damage had already started to calcify. Conversations turned into arguments. Then silence. James began missing dinners. Then birthdays. And finally, just... moments. The ones that mattered most.

He didn't know how to fix it. But he tried. In his own flawed, blustering way. The weekend trip was part of that attempt. James had borrowed a friend's fishing cabin up near Liberty Reservoir. It was supposed to be a clean break. No phones. No sirens. Just father and son, fresh air, and time. Maybe catch a few bass. Maybe catch up on all the years that had slipped through their fingers like sand.

"Let's make this weekend count, son," James had said that morning, his voice rough with a rare tenderness. It was the first time in what felt like years that they had a genuine plan. Just the two of them. A movie later. A little fishing out at Liberty Reservoir.

Ribs from that hole-in-the-wall on Greenmount that always smelled like smoke and heaven. A future, however fragile, seemed to shimmer on the horizon. But first the liquor store. Always the liquor store. A quick stop, James had promised, just to grab something for the cabin. A familiar ritual, a minor detour in the grand plan.

James pulled the Crown Vic into a faded parking spot in front of a corner shop that looked like it had been built to survive a war. Bars on the windows. Cameras with cracked lenses, blind eyes watching the street. A heavy metal door that stuck, groaning on its hinges. He flicked his half-smoked Newport out the window, the cherry glowing briefly on the hot asphalt, and gave Marcus a confident grin. "Just a quick stop," he said. "Be right back, my son. Don't go nowhere."

Marcus nodded, pretending not to mind the delay. He knew the drill. Patience was a virtue, especially with James. Inside the stifling car, he tapped a rhythm on the dashboard, mimicking the infectious beat of a popular rap track playing in his mind. He watched his father swagger toward the store that confident, almost lazy gait he always had, shoulders back, a slight roll to his step.

James disappeared inside, the doorbell chiming with a sharp, almost ominous jangle. The store's fluorescent lights buzzed overhead as James approached the counter. The clerk, a skinny man with pale skin and darting, nervous eyes, glared the moment James walked in. This wasn't the usual easygoing guy James bantered with; this was a stranger, twitchy and suspicious. His eyes dropped to the bulge beneath James's loose button-down a holstered Glock, regulation-issue. James, oblivious to the clerk's sudden tension, reached behind the counter for a bottle of Erk & Jerk, a familiar brand he'd grabbed a hundred times before.

The clerk flinched, a subtle movement, but enough. Outside, Marcus sat back, the quiet thrum of the neighborhood filling the silence. A man cursed from somewhere up the block, the words like shattered glass. A baby cried behind the thin walls of a nearby rowhouse, its wail a lonely counterpoint to the heat. Marcus barely noticed. The rhythm in his head pulsed louder, a shield against the heavy air.

He thought about the last time they'd gone fishing. It had been so long, years, since they'd cast lines together. James had taught him how to bait a hook, how to cast without tangling the line, how to wait with quiet patience for the tug. That day came back to him in flashes: the glint of sunlight off the water, the earthy smell of bait, the quiet pride in his father's eyes when Marcus reeled in his first catch a smallmouth bass, ugly but glorious. He wondered if today would be like that again. If they could reclaim something. If they could just *be* father and son, without the static of their fractured lives.

Then came the sirens. Not distant. Not idle. Close. Too close. He sat up straight, his breath catching in his throat. His eyes scanned the street frantically. A cruiser screamed into the parking lot, tires screeching as they braked hard and scattered loose gravel across the pavement. Blue and red lights pulsed, painting the cracked asphalt in a violent, urgent strobe. Officers spilled out guns already drawn, glinting with a cold, metallic hunger.

Marcus froze, his blood turning to ice. One of the cops was a towering white man, square-jawed with a buzz cut and a red, angry face that looked born of rage. His nameplate, Marcus could just make it out, read: GRAYFORD. He shouted first, his voice ripping through the air like a gunshot.

"GET ON THE GROUND! NOW! HANDS WHERE I CAN SEE THEM!"

Marcus's pulse roared in his ears, a frantic drumbeat against his skull. He looked toward the store just as his father stepped out, the paper bag with the bottle clutched in his hand.

"What the...?" James blinked against the blinding sun, clearly disoriented, caught off guard. He raised his free hand, palm open, a gesture of confusion, not aggression. "What's going on?"

"DOWN! HANDS WHERE I CAN SEE THEM!" Grayford bellowed again, his weapon leveled.

James hesitated, startled by the ferocity, the raw aggression in the officer's voice. The paper bag in his right hand crinkled loudly. He raised his left hand higher, instinctively trying to de-escalate.

"I'm a cop," he said, his voice laced with the authority of his badge, even as it quivered with surprise. "I'm—"

His hand moved.

Not toward the bottle.

Not toward a threat.

Toward his badge, holstered at his hip, a motion born of instinct, of training, of a desire to identify himself. Two shots cracked the sky, impossibly loud, ripping through the humid air. James twisted, a shocked gasp escaping his lips. The bottle flew from his hand, shattering on the pavement with a sickening splash. His knees buckled, the sudden loss of life force stealing his strength. He fell face-first onto the concrete, the badge still half-visible, glinting mockingly in his lifeless grip. Bourbon and blood spilled together, mixing into a dark, sticky pool that spread across the thirsty pavement.

Marcus couldn't move. His body was a statue of horror, rooted to the passenger seat. Grayford stood over the body, his chest rising and falling like he'd just won a brutal fight, a thin sheen of sweat on his brow. The other officer a young Black man named Kevin Mitchell, his face pale with shock lowered his weapon slowly, his eyes wide, fixed on James's prone form. "He was reaching for his badge," Kevin said, his voice barely a whisper, laced with disbelief and dawning horror.

"He threatened the clerk," Grayford snapped, his voice sharp, defensive, cutting off Mitchell's protest. "We didn't see a badge. We saw movement. A threat. He went for his weapon."

Marcus heard every word. Felt every syllable like glass in his throat, each one a shard of the collapsing world. They didn't know he was there. Hidden in plain sight, a witness to a truth they would bury. He slouched lower in the seat, pressing himself against the hot vinyl, eyes locked on the blood creeping across the pavement like a slow, dark tide. A weight settled in his chest, heavy and permanent, colder than any ice. It was the weight of knowing, of witnessing, of a silence that screamed.

Drew James's longtime partner, a man whose laughter had always filled the precinct arrived on the scene minutes later, but it felt like an eternity. His unmarked car screeched to a halt, tires smoking. He ran toward the body, his face contorted in disbelief, then horror.

"No. No... James!" He yelled, a raw, primal scream torn from his gut, tears streaming down his face as he knelt beside his fallen friend.

Drew turned to Grayford, his voice thick with grief and fury. "He was a cop, dammit! Your brother in blue! You didn't recognize him?"

"We saw a threat," Grayford said, his voice flat, devoid of emotion. "We followed protocol. Standard procedure."

"He was your brother in blue, Grayford! How could you not" Grayford didn't blink. "We feared for our lives. He made a move. End of story."

Drew scanned the chaos, his eyes searching, desperate, until they locked with Marcus's, still slumped in the Crown Vic. A flicker of understanding, then fierce protectiveness, crossed Drew's face. He rushed to the car, yanking the door open.

"Marcus! Are you hurt? Are you okay? Son, speak to me!"

Marcus didn't answer. Couldn't. He was somewhere else. Somewhere passed screaming. Past crying. He was in a quiet, burning space where everything had changed. Drew, quick-thinking amidst the chaos, snuck Marcus to his own car. With the flashing lights, the gathering crowd, the other officers preoccupied, it was tragically easy to do.

He covered Marcus with a blanket, a desperate attempt to shield him from the horror, from the eyes of the world. Drew left the scene in a haste, driving young Marcus back home. He was talking to Marcus, a stream of questions, reassurances, but got zero response. No tears, no emotion, just a dead, glazed-over stare that chilled Drew to the bone. The boy was gone, replaced by a ghost.

They walked through the door. Veronica, wiping flour from her hands, looked at Marcus, puzzled. "Boy, y'all trip ended that quickly? James drop you off?" Her voice held the usual sarcastic edge, unaware of the abyss opening before them. Drew, his face ashen, quickly stepped in behind Marcus. "V," he began, his voice cracking. "There was an incident. It's… it's James."

11

Veronica's eyes widened, a dawning comprehension twisting her features. "They shot him? James? James is dead?!" Her voice rose to a shriek, a raw sound of disbelief and agony that tore through the small house. Marcus sat curled in on himself on the worn living room sofa. He heard nothing. Not the screams. Not the sirens, now faint and distant. Just the shots. Over and over.

The precise, terrible rhythm of the two cracks that had cleaved his world in two. The moment James reached for his badge. The moment the world ended. Drew knelt in front of him, his eyes pleading, desperate to penetrate the wall Marcus had erected.

"Marcus. What did you see, son? Please. Tell me."

Marcus looked up, his face blank, his eyes like polished stones. "They lied," he said, his voice flat, devoid of inflection, a chilling pronouncement.

Drew swallowed hard, his own grief momentarily forgotten, replaced by a cold dread. "Tell me what happened, Marcus. Every detail."

"He told them who he was," Marcus whispered, the words barely audible. "He showed them his badge. They didn't care." Silence fell again.

A silence that would last for years, stretching like an unbroken wire through his adolescence. And inside it, Marcus Caldwell made a vow, a silent, burning promise etched onto his soul:

Justice wouldn't wear a badge. It would wear his name.

Chapter Two

The Transformation

The funeral came in a blur of black suits and tear-streaked faces. The church was packed beyond capacity cops in dress blues, their brass gleaming mockingly, neighbors, extended family, even strangers who only knew James Caldwell by the shadow he left in their community, now gone. The air buzzed with a heavy mix of grief and confusion. Rumors had already begun to swirl like predatory birds. Some whispered it was a tragic mistake. Others, bolder, more defiant, hissed it was murder.

Marcus sat near the front beside his mother, his hands clenched in his lap, nails digging into his palms. He didn't cry. He couldn't. The tears felt locked behind a wall of ice, too rigid to break. Not even when they folded the flag with precise, ceremonial movements and handed it to Veronica, who nearly collapsed in her seat, her sobs echoing through the solemn sanctuary. Not when the minister praised James's integrity, his service, the very ideals that had been shattered. Not when the bagpipes began their slow, mournful wail, a sound that should have torn him apart. His eyes were dry, but inside, a storm raged. A silent, churning vortex of disbelief, pain, and a nascent, terrifying resolve.

He studied the officers in attendance. He saw Drew, red-eyed, jaw set like concrete, a man grappling with his own loyalty and heartbreak. He saw Kevin Mitchell, lingering at the edge of the crowd, a ghost of guilt written all over his pale face. And he saw Grayford, standing stiffly beside his captain, emotionless behind his dark aviators, a predator hiding in plain sight.

Marcus's gaze burned through him, a silent, unacknowledged challenge. He committed Grayford's impassive face to memory, carving it into the deepest, coldest part of his being. That night, Marcus lay in bed, staring at the ceiling. The fan above him spun in slow, lazy circles, doing little to push away the humid, crushing weight of the room.

He listened to his mother crying softly down the hall, her grief a low, constant hum that resonated in his bones. Every muffled sob, every choked breath, cut deeper than any knife.

He got up, driven by an ache he couldn't name, and walked to his father's closet. He opened it slowly, as if disturbing a sacred tomb. The scent hit him immediately Joop. It clung to the collar of his dress shirts, the lining of his old blazer, the faint, lingering essence of the man who was no longer there. It was the smell of every memory Marcus had from childhood the scent James wore when he took Veronica dancing, when he showed up to school recitals, when things were still okay, still whole.

Marcus inhaled it like he was breathing in the past, drawing strength from the fading echo of a life. Like if he stood there long enough, rooted in that scent, his father would walk through the door again, the jangle of keys, the familiar booming voice. But the door never opened. His father's badge case sat on the dresser, untouched since his mother had carefully put it away. Marcus picked it up, the cool metal heavy in his palm, and slowly opened it. The gold shield gleamed, a symbol of honor now tarnished by blood and lies.

Caldwell. James E. Detective, BPD.

His own reflection stared back at him in the polished metal, a grim, determined young face, eyes already too old for his years. He didn't just lose his father that day. He lost the world he once believed in. The world where justice wore a badge, where heroes were protected, where truth eventually prevailed. That world had shattered into a million irreparable pieces.

In the days that followed, he became a ghost in his own home. Veronica tried to reach him, her voice thick with worry and desperate love, but every time she opened her mouth, Marcus was already somewhere else physically present, a silent, brooding presence, but emotionally buried with his father. So he went quiet. The once lively chatter, the occasional teenage angst, the laughter all ceased. But silence didn't mean stillness. It meant focus. An intense, singular sharpening of purpose. It meant birth. The agonizing, relentless birth of something new, something dangerous.

Days blurred into weeks, then months. Friends came and went, their awkward condolences and well-meaning invitations falling flat against the wall he'd erected. Food piled in the fridge, untouched. Cards lined the mantle, their sentiments hollow. But Marcus stayed quiet. He avoided calls. He told his mother he wasn't up to going back to school yet, the very thought of classrooms and superficial chatter nauseating him. He slept when he could, his dreams a tortured replay of the incident, and woke up to nightmares that bled into the harsh light of day.

He kept replaying it. The look on James's face surprise, confusion, then utter disbelief. The way Grayford raised his gun like it was second nature, a detached, mechanical movement. The silence that followed the shots, a deafening void where his father's life had been. That summer, while other kids took road trips, hit basketball courts, or worked part-time jobs at the mall, Marcus waged a private war. A war not against others, but within himself, transforming grief into fuel.

Marcus spent his summer break devouring everything he could find books on law enforcement protocols, criminal psychology, surveillance tech, encryption, and hacking. He studied not to pass tests, but to build a toolkit for dismantling the very systems that had failed his father. He read Sun Tzu's *The Art of War*, Machiavelli's *The Prince*, and dissected every revenge plot in literature and film, from *The Count of Monte Cristo* to *John Wick*. He consumed documentaries on corporate espionage and government cover-ups, seeing the hidden levers of power.

Then he started going further. Beyond academic pursuit. He created registered dummy accounts, untraceable digital footprints. He visited forums where cops and ex-cops posted anonymously, gleaning insights into internal politics, grudges, and unspoken rules. He learned the jargon, the unwritten codes, the vulnerabilities.

He read books on internal investigations, use-of-force protocols, the politics of cover-ups, the art of misdirection. Over the next few years, Marcus wouldn't just become educated he was becoming dangerous. A quiet, cerebral threat. He knew how evidence disappeared. How digital trails were scrubbed clean.

How stories got rewritten, official narratives crafted to protect the powerful. How systems protected their own, closing ranks against inconvenient truths.

His body transformed in tandem with his mind, a physical manifestation of his deepening resolve. He trained with the fury of a soldier denied a battlefield. He did pushups until failure, shadowboxing in the dark, picturing Grayford's face with every jab, running before dawn with ankle weights and vengeance in his chest, the Baltimore streets his unforgiving track. His diet shifted from comfort food to pure fuel, his muscles hardened into sinewy steel, and every bead of sweat was a drop of his old, innocent self leaving him, burning away the weakness.

The boy who loved Saturday Morning Cartoons and Sunday pancakes, who had a tentative crush on the girl two blocks over, had slowly died. What rose from that grave was a tactician. A machine built for vengeance. Justice for his slain father. A quiet, unstoppable force.

Chapter Three

The First Meeting

Marcus began frequenting the neighborhood again but not like before. He moved with a new awareness, a sharpened perception. He listened more than he spoke, his ears finely tuned to the rhythms of the streets, the unspoken truths. He lingered in barbershops and corner stores, overhearing whispers, piecing together rumors and resentments like fragments of a shattered mirror.

A local street prophet named Old Sam sat outside the bus stop every day, muttering about devils in blue and hidden tapes, his voice raspy, his eyes too knowing. "You see somethin' they don't want seen, they make sure your mouth stay shut," Sam said, his gaze distant but piercing. "But they don't know how to kill memory. That's where revolution lives."

Marcus started writing that down too. Every cryptic phrase, every forgotten detail, every name. He had begun keeping a notebook, its pages filled with neat, precise script. Not just facts. Not just plans.

Manifestos. A blueprint for a reckoning. It was around this time that Marcus made his first deliberate approach to the physical world, a world where the stakes were measured in blood and bone, not just bytes and whispers.

He walked into a boxing gym on North Avenue, the heavy scent of sweat, old canvas, and hard lessons hitting him like a physical blow. The rhythmic thump of a speed bag, the grunt of effort, the sharp crack of leather on a heavy bag—it was a symphony of controlled violence. "You train fighters here?" Marcus asked the grizzled man behind the counter, a man whose face was a roadmap of old scars and weathered wisdom. "We train men who don't wanna stay broken," the man said, his voice raspy, his eyes appraising Marcus with a look that saw beyond the polite façade. "We teach 'em how to stand up when the world tries to knock 'em down."

"Good," Marcus said, his voice quiet but firm. "That's what I need." Marcus's training at the gym became its own brutal ritual, a crucible. He showed up early and stayed late, studying every move, every counter, every subtle shift in weight. The man behind the counter Manny Torres had once been a Golden Gloves champ before a knee injury ended his shot at the pros. What remained was a man carved from grit, with a voice like sandpaper and fists like cinder blocks, still capable of moving with startling speed for his age.

Manny didn't ask too many questions about Marcus's past, but he watched him carefully. He saw the way the kid threw himself into the work not just with discipline, but with a raw, desperate intensity that spoke of something deeper than ambition. Marcus fought like he was trying to tear down a building with his bare hands. "You trying to fight somebody, son?" Manny asked one evening, after a particularly grueling session where Marcus had pushed himself past exhaustion. "I'm trying to fight everybody," Marcus said without looking up, sweat stinging his eyes.

Manny grunted, a sound of reluctant approval. "Then you better learn to breathe between hits. Revenge don't mean shit if you get knocked out in the first round. You gotta have a long game in this life, kid. A real long game."

At home, Veronica made sure to stay strong for Marcus. She moved through the house with a quiet grace, her grief a contained storm beneath her calm surface. She worked extra shifts, kept the house immaculate, tried to maintain some semblance of normalcy in a world that had none. Although years had passed, she continued to try and reassure Marcus that everything would be alright. That life would find its way back to them. But her eyes carried a perpetual sadness, a deep, unhealing wound.

Marcus remembered the nights he would lie awake, listening to his mother talking to James's picture, a framed photograph on her nightstand, when she thought Marcus couldn't hear. How she would sometimes curse him for leaving, for the chaos he left behind. Other times she pleaded with him to come back, her voice raw with longing.

And when she wasn't speaking to the photo, she was silent for hours, lost in a grief that was too vast for words. He recalled, once, she tried to make Marcus talk. Sat him down at the kitchen table with tear-glossed eyes and trembling hands, a desperate plea in her voice.

"We can't fall apart," she'd said, her voice barely a whisper. "He wouldn't want that for us. Not for you, baby."

He remembered nodding, not because he agreed, not because the words held any comfort, but because he didn't know how to say: *I've already fallen. I'm just learning how to land.* One day, almost instinctively, Marcus returned to the corner store where it all happened. The glass had been replaced, the storefront painted over, but the scars remained, visible only to him. A new clerk stood behind the counter, oblivious to the history etched into the very foundations of the building. But the ghosts remained, swirling in the oppressive heat, whispering of shattered glass and spilled blood.

He lingered outside, watching the camera above the door, its cracked lens a silent witness. Remembering. Every detail, every second.

A man walked by, his face lined with the weariness of the streets, and gave Marcus a knowing nod. Marcus simply nodded back, a flicker of understanding passing between them. "World's full of cowards with guns," the man muttered, walking off, his voice a gravelly echo. "Ain't no justice coming unless you bring it yourself."

Marcus watched him go, the words hanging in the stagnant air, confirming a truth he already held. That night, he dreamed of the shooting again. The familiar horror, the gut-wrenching helplessness. But this time, in the dream, he moved. This time, he got out of the car. Screamed. Fought. Took the bullet instead. And woke up gasping, drenched in sweat, the phantom pain in his chest too real.

The following afternoon, Baltimore's heat still baking the sidewalk, shimmering off the asphalt when a black Escalade, gleaming like a predator in the sun, crept silently beside him. It was too sleek, too quiet for this part of town.

"Hey, Marcus?" a voice called out, smooth as polished obsidian. He turned, guarded, every muscle tensed for flight or fight.

The tinted window slid down with a whisper, revealing a man mid-thirties, lean and clean, with a meticulously trimmed goatee, two diamond studs gleaming subtly in his ears, and a sharpness in his gaze that made the air feel heavier, charged with unspoken power. "Hop in," the man said, his voice a low command, not a request. "Let's talk."

Marcus hesitated. The Escalade gleamed like temptation, like a promise of something far beyond the grimy streets, but the man inside didn't radiate recklessness. He radiated command, a quiet, undeniable authority. Every fiber of Marcus's carefully honed instinct screamed danger, but another part, the part hungry for more, recognized an opportunity. Marcus opened the door and climbed in. The soft hum of the engine, the conditioned air, felt like stepping into another world.

Inside, the air smelled of fine leather, subtle cologne, and power. Not the brute force power of Grayford, but something more refined, more dangerous. "I'm Damon," the man said, driving slow, one hand on the wheel, the other resting with casual confidence on the console. "People talk, Marcus. Teachers. Streets. You got something most kids don't. I know about your pops.

That shit…" He paused, letting the weight of the unspoken hang in the air. "Pain like that, it either breaks you or builds you. Looks like it built you into something formidable."

"I have been watching you for the last few years, Marcus," Damon continued, his voice low, almost a purr. "Watching how you move, how you learn, how you hold yourself. And what I see, is someone I can use. Someone who understands discipline. Someone who understands vengeance."

Marcus didn't reply. He didn't have to. The silence itself was an answer, a mutual understanding. Damon turned a corner and pulled into a deserted alley, then shifted the SUV into park, the engine ticking softly. The sudden quiet felt immense. "I'm not asking you to sling rock or hold guns," Damon said, turning to face Marcus fully, his eyes holding an unnerving intensity. "I don't need corner boys. I need chess players. Minds. Strategists. I see one in you. So, I'll ask you again, Marcus: You in?"

Marcus studied him, his gaze unwavering. Marcus knew exactly who Damon Hughes was. A ghost story whispered on the streets, a legend born of ambition and ruthless efficiency. He knew what Damon was capable of. And he knew what he wanted. "I want information," Marcus said coldly, his voice flat, emotionless. "On the cops who killed my father. Especially Harold Grayford. I want everything."

Damon smiled slowly, a predatory, knowing curve of his lips, like a man seeing a reflection of his younger, hungrier self.

"Deal," Damon said, extending a hand. The handshake was firm, a silent pact forged in the heat of a Baltimore summer.

DAMON: THE PRODIGY FROM PENN-NORTH

Damon Hughes came from a different kind of hunger. Not the one that clawed at your stomach though he'd known that too, intimately, as a child but the one that sat in your chest, a relentless whisper: *More. Be more. Rise above.* His mother, Tasha, worked double shifts as a CNA, her hands raw, her back aching, her spirit unbroken. She never took a day off. Never missed a rent payment. Raised her boys alone in a cramped apartment near Penn-North, where the paint peeled from the walls and mice scurried like ghosts at night. Damon worshipped her. He and his younger brother, Terrell, shared a bunk bed and a dream: to take care of the woman who had sacrificed everything for them. Damon wasn't book-smart in school, not in the traditional sense, but he was life-smart. He saw things. Patterns. Weaknesses. Angles. He understood human nature better than any textbook could teach.

By thirteen, he'd knocked out a boy twice his size in a playground brawl, not with brute strength, but with precise, unexpected movements. By fourteen, he was fighting grown men in alleyway matches for money—bare-knuckle, no rules, no mercy, his quick mind calculating vulnerabilities, his body moving with a predatory grace.

He hustled chess in Druid Hill Park, setting up boards under the shade and baiting older men into betting fifty-dollar bills. They laughed when he moved his first pawn, dismissing him as a child. They didn't laugh after they lost in nine moves, their faces stunned, their pockets lighter. He read the greats by flashlight Malcolm X, Huey Newton, Miyamoto Musashi absorbing their fire and precision, their philosophies of power and resistance.

He didn't see gangsters as role models. He saw generals, strategists in a brutal urban warfare. Damon didn't want fast money. He wanted dominance. Stability. A dynasty. He got into the dope game the way other kids joined basketball leagues. Calculated. Reluctant at first, seeing it as a means, not an end. Focused. He studied supply chains, distribution networks, human frailties.

He built small first, one corner, a handful of runners, no flashy cars, no Instagram displays of wealth. He didn't touch drugs, didn't use. Kept clean. Kept quiet. He lived modestly, reinvesting every cent.

By seventeen, he was running half the west-side of Baltimore like a finely tuned Swiss timepiece, a silent, efficient machine. He was sending his younger brother, Terrell, to college at Morgan State on the money, a promise kept, a future secured. By twenty, he'd franchised that hustle into an underground empire, a network that stretched across the city. He laundered his cash through legitimate channels: real estate flips, black-owned businesses, even grant-funded charities, blurring the lines between illicit and legitimate wealth.

He paid off cops. Bought politicians. Helped build churches. His influence seeped into every stratum of the city. But he never forgot who he was. Or where he came from. Every move was for his mother. Every step a brick in his dynasty.

THE EDUCATION OF MARCUS

Damon didn't just take Marcus under his wing he sharpened him like a blade, honing every nascent skill, every raw instinct. He gave him a secure laptop, a military-grade VPN, and access to private forums where whistleblowers, ex-fed contractors, and digital ghosts exchanged secrets, trading in information too volatile for the public eye.

Marcus learned from ex-hackers who could penetrate any firewall, corporate accountants turned rogue who knew where every hidden ledger lay, and former spooks whose names were scrubbed from government records, masters of surveillance and counter-intelligence. They taught him how to trace dirty money through shell corporations, write untraceable code, scrub metadata from video and audio files, and plant digital breadcrumbs that led nowhere but a dead end.

But Damon also demanded physical discipline. He understood that true power required a body as sharp as the mind. Each morning, Marcus met a rotation of brutal instructors: former MMA fighters whose fists were lethal weapons, retired military operators with a chilling economy of motion, and street-slick brawlers who taught the ugly, effective truth of urban combat. He learned to strike with bone-shattering force, grapple with suffocating control, disarm with blinding speed, and endure pain with stoic resolve. Muay Thai. Krav Maga. Jiu-jitsu. He was no longer just fit he was a fucking beast, a coiled spring of controlled aggression.

Damon watched it all from the shadows, a silent, assessing presence, measuring Marcus's progress, testing his limits. "You're not just learning to survive, Marcus," Damon said one night, after Marcus had pushed himself to exhaustion in the gym, his muscles screaming. "You're learning to command. To dominate. To inflict your will on the world." Marcus nodded, breathing hard, his eyes reflecting the cold, hard light of the gym. A weapon was being forged in fire. And it was nearly complete.

Chapter Four

The Infiltration

By the time the new school year began, Marcus Caldwell had become unrecognizable. The boy who had sat slumped in the Crown Vic, broken and silent, had vanished. To the world, he was a standout. A star student, his grades impeccable.

A rising athlete, his raw talent refined into explosive power on the basketball court. The golden boy from Baltimore, lifted by scholarship, destined for something brighter, a beacon of hope for his community. But beneath the surface, he was something far more dangerous, far more complex. He was a soldier in plain clothes. A ghost moving through the bright halls of privilege. And he had already chosen his battlefield: the heart of the system that had destroyed his family.

Marcus enrolled at Worthington High, a polished, predominantly white prep school nestled in a well-manicured neighborhood far from the sirens and sagging power lines of his own. The scholarship came from one of Damon's shell charities "For Future Kings" a name as ironic as it was prophetic, given the king Marcus was becoming, and the king he was planning to unseat.

He moved through the hallways like a shadow in a tailored uniform, observing everything, betraying nothing. Teachers praised his intellect, his thoughtful insights, his quiet intensity. Coaches marveled at his explosiveness on the court, his natural leadership. Students whispered about his style, his strength, his intriguing mystery the new kid who seemed to appear from nowhere, radiating an unspoken power.

He was the perfect blend of hunger and polish, an enigma wrapped in an expensive blazer. And that's precisely what drew Karen Grayford in.

The Rise of a Scholar-Athlete

From the outside, Marcus's transformation looked like a miracle a testament to resilience and hard work. But it was built on blood, sweat, and obsessive discipline. Each day was a carefully constructed ritual of self-mastery.

He woke every morning before sunrise, running five miles through the cracked sidewalks of his neighborhood before heading to the gym. His workouts were brutal— battle ropes that coiled like pythons, hill sprints that burned his lungs, deadlifts that tested the limits of his strength, explosive footwork drills that turned him into a blur. He sculpted his body like a statue of vengeance: lean, powerful, precise, capable of both brutal force and silent infiltration.

Every movement had a purpose.

Every rep was a promise to his father's grave, a drop of sweat sealing the vow. After training, he devoured his coursework with the same relentless intensity AP Calculus that bent to his will, college-level writing seminars where his prose cut like a scalpel, forensic science electives that taught him the language of evidence and its manipulation. He wasn't studying for grades. He was collecting tools, weapons for the coming war.

In the evenings, he shadowboxed in his room under flickering light, perfecting every strike, every block, every takedown. Then he sat cross-legged on the floor, surrounded by glowing screens, reading case law, deconstructing SWAT protocols, and running backdoor scripts into the public record servers of Baltimore PD, mapping their vulnerabilities. He studied everything.

Including her.

Karen Grayford

She moved like someone who'd never needed to worry, her posture effortlessly graceful, her laughter light and unburdened. Daughter of Harold Grayford, the cop who murdered Marcus's father. The architect of his nightmare.

Blond, graceful, and outspoken about social causes, Karen was the kind of girl who thought herself woke because she posted James Baldwin quotes over filtered selfies and retweeted injustice from the safety of a suburban Wi-Fi signal. Her outrage was intellectual and detached.

Marcus found her online months before he ever spoke to her, sifting through her digital footprint with meticulous care. He knew her playlist, indie folk mixed with conscious hip-hop. Her favorite coffee order, a Venti Iced Latte with almond milk and a shot of vanilla.

That she was heartbroken when Kendrick didn't win Album of the Year. That she cried when George Floyd died, her online posts filled with performative anguish, but never once questioned the badge on her father's chest, never linked his profession to the systemic issues she decried. She wasn't evil. She was ignorant. Privileged. Naive. And that made her useful. A key to the front door.

The Setup

Their first meeting wasn't fate. It wasn't accidental. It was stagecraft. A meticulously orchestrated scene. He spotted her at The Olive Branch Café, a small off-campus joint she frequented every Thursday afternoon for her study group. Damon had someone subtly reserve the table next to hers, ensuring their proximity. Marcus made sure to wear a worn, comfortable hoodie with a profound Langston Hughes quote subtly printed on the back strategically visible when he "accidentally" bumped her tray, sending her organic smoothie wobbling. "Sorry about that," he said, flashing a shy, rehearsed smile, his eyes holding a carefully cultivated innocence. Karen looked up from her smoothie, annoyed at first, then curious, her gaze catching on the words on his back. "You know Langston Hughes?" she asked, a flicker of surprise and interest in her eyes. "He saved my life," Marcus replied, the lie so smooth it tasted like truth, a perfect blend of vulnerability and artistic depth.

From there, it was easy. A carefully curated escalation of contact. Texts that started with apologies and drifted into shared interests. Lunches in the bustling cafeteria that became their own private world. Study sessions that bled into late-night FaceTimes, conversations stretching into the pre-dawn hours.

She was smart, idealistic, but profoundly lonely, craving genuine connection amidst the superficiality of her privileged world. Her father was always working, distant and preoccupied. Her mother was cold, wrapped in her own world of suburban anxieties. Karen liked the way Marcus listened, truly listened. The way he looked at her like she was the only one who mattered, like he saw something deeper than anyone else.

She didn't know she was a mark. She thought she'd found a soulmate.

The Infiltration Begins

Karen, unknowingly, invited him into her world one fragile piece at a time. A party here, full of the polite chatter of the wealthy elite. A casual family dinner there, Marcus observing Harold with a quiet, burning intensity, a perfect blend of respect and simmering hatred.

Soon, Marcus was sitting at the pristine dining table, shaking Harold Grayford's hand, his smile polite, his eyes carefully blank, hiding the fire in his chest every time the man spoke, every time he saw his father's killer laugh, oblivious.

Harold didn't recognize him. Why would he? To Harold, the boy in the car that day had been a shadow, a blip, a negligible detail in a messy incident. Not even worth a report, let alone a second thought. But Marcus remembered everything. The way the blood pooled. The cold precision in Grayford's eyes. He planted a keystroke logger on Harold's office desktop during a bathroom break, a quick, practiced movement. Installed a wireless receiver under the router in the Grayford family's impeccably decorated living room on his third visit, a tiny, almost invisible parasite. Synced Harold's personal and work emails to a secure offshore server within two weeks, a silent, ceaseless stream of data flowing directly to Marcus's encrypted drive.

When Karen kissed him goodnight, her lips soft and trusting, he smiled, a ghost of a smile that never reached his eyes. When she, sweet and naive, whispered "I love you," he kissed her forehead, a platonic gesture, already planning his next move.

But when she fell asleep, curled innocently beside him after a movie night, he put in noise-canceling earbuds, pulled out his discreet laptop, and harvested the secrets of the man who'd destroyed his life, his fingers flying across the keyboard with cold, surgical precision.

The Smoking Gun

One night, the universe, or perhaps fate, offered a gift. Harold, unusually careless, left his work tablet unlocked on the kitchen counter after a late-night conference call.

Marcus excused himself to "grab water," his movements fluid and silent. In less than 90 seconds, his heart a steady drumbeat, he connected a tiny, disguised USB drive and copied over the entire directory of Harold's restricted folders. Every file. Every encrypted document. Hours later, alone in his darkened bedroom, the only light the glow from his screen, he found it: "Red Flag: Edgewood Incident." A folder full of silence and sin, carefully buried, meticulously redacted:

- Redacted 911 transcripts, crucial moments of the call conspicuously absent.

- Body cam footage, cut by over two minutes, erasing Grayford's aggression, James's attempt at identification.

- Forensic photos with forged timestamps, carefully manipulated to alter the timeline.

- Original statements overwritten by "clean" versions, the truth scrubbed, replaced by palatable lies. It was all there. The irrefutable, undeniable proof of the cover-up.

Proof of the lie that had shattered his family, murdered his father, and twisted his own life into a weapon. Marcus stared at the files, eyes hollow, the images burning themselves into his mind. The cold, blue glow from the screen reflected off the scar tissue in his soul, illuminating the path forward. "Got you," he whispered, the words a silent, chilling promise in the stillness of the night.

But he didn't press send. Not yet. Because revenge was never the finish line. Not for Marcus Caldwell. It was just one piece of a larger storm, a single opening salvo in a war he intended to win.

The Inner Harbor Conversation

That weekend, Damon summoned him to the penthouse, a silent, urgent summons that Marcus instinctively obeyed. The elevator opened directly into a sprawling, open-concept suite overlooking the Baltimore Inner Harbor. Floor-to-ceiling windows painted the city in a shifting tableau of gold and deepening twilight, the lights of the city glittering like scattered diamonds. Whiskey shelves lined one wall, gleaming bottles catching the light.

A massive, complex map with red pins and string, a spiderweb of influence and power, covered another. Damon stood in front of it, sipping Suntory whiskey, a silhouette against the vibrant city. "Tell me what you've found," he said, without turning, his voice calm, expectant.

Marcus laid the drive on the polished glass table, a tiny, innocuous object holding a universe of damning truth. "Everything. The whole damn cover-up. Grayford's involved from the ground up." Damon exhaled slowly through his nose, a puff of air that held years of cynical understanding. "I figured. Cops like that don't stop. They rot from the inside out. They believe their uniform gives them impunity."

Marcus walked toward the map, his gaze sweeping over it, noticing new pins. New strings. Areas he hadn't seen before, connections that stretched beyond the usual street-level operations. "What's all this?" he asked, a subtle shift in his focus. Damon took a long sip, then turned, his eyes piercing through the dim light, catching Marcus's gaze.

"This," he said, a slow, deliberate cadence in his voice, "is power. My power. And someone's trying to take it from me. Someone within my own ranks."Marcus narrowed his eyes, a name already forming. "Reggie?" Damon's jaw flexed, a subtle tightening of muscle. "That's what I need you to confirm. And then, eliminate." Marcus looked again at the intricate web of strings and names, a map of alliances and betrayals. The city. The empire Damon had painstakingly built. The insidious betrayal within its very heart.

There were battles to fight in the open.

And wars to win in the shadows. He was ready for both.

Chapter five

Smoke Beneath the Throne

The war had begun, but there were no headlines, no flashing lights, no public declarations. Only whispers carried on the wind, the sudden disappearance of known faces, empty chairs at the poker table where deals were cut. And somewhere deep inside Damon's sprawling empire, Reggie Sykes, a man blinded by ambition and a warped sense of entitlement, was making his moves. He was careful. Patient. Calculating.

But not careful enough. Not for Marcus.

A Soft Betrayal

It was Marcus who noticed first. He wasn't looking for betrayal he was cataloguing the business like a living algorithm, his mind a vast, intricate network of data points.

He tracked operations: drops, deposits, movement, messaging. He saw the patterns, the predictable ebb and flow of Damon's flawlessly constructed enterprise. Then a new pattern emerged silent, subtle, a discordant note in the symphony of efficiency.

Money that disappeared from ledgers without explanation. Soldiers moved to new territories without Damon's explicit order. New faces appearing on old corners, their loyalties unverified. Conversations that stopped abruptly when certain people entered the room, a sudden, unnatural hush.

Marcus followed it like a thread pulled through a fresh wound a slow, insidious unraveling. And every strand, every anomaly, led back to Reggie. He was building something on the side. A crew. A splinter cell. An empire within an empire, fueled by arrogance and a hunger that mirrored Damon's own, but lacked the vision.

Karen: The Obsession and the Weapon

While Damon's empire shifted precariously beneath him, Marcus pulled Karen deeper into his world, closer to the illusion he had so carefully crafted closer to the trap he was setting for her father. Yet, she had become more than just a means to an end. She was his solace, his momentary comfort, the only person who made him almost forget the crushing weight of what he carried. Almost. One Friday night, they lay in her bed, the expensive sheets cool against their skin.

The room was lit only by her softly glowing lava lamp and the ambient glow of city lights spilling through her blinds. A slow jam played in the background silky vocals, deep bass, the kind of track designed for bodies pressed together, for whispers and tangled limbs.Karen was curled into Marcus's chest, her fingers drawing invisible patterns across his stomach, her breath soft against his skin. "This song," she whispered, her voice thick with emotion, "it makes me feel... everything.

Like we're the only two people in the world."He didn't speak. He just leaned in, kissed her lips—softly at first, then deeper, drawing her breath into his own, tasting the sweetness of her trust, the bitterness of his deception. The song faded into the background as her breath grew shallow, quickening. Their lips danced, slow and deliberate. His hands slid beneath the hem of her dress, gliding over her thighs with practiced control, a touch that promised intimacy, masking a colder intent. When his finger found her center, she gasped—hips lifting instinctively, a soft, involuntary moan escaping her throat. "M-Marcus…" she moaned, her voice cracking like glass, trembling with arousal. He didn't stop. He pressed against her clit in slow, delicate circles, watching her eyes flutter closed, her head falling back against the pillow.

Her moans filled the air like a desperate prayer, a testament to his calculated touch. He lifted her shirt, his gaze briefly sweeping over her. Her breasts, soft and perfectly perky, rose and fell with every quickening breath. He took one into his mouth, sucked gently, teasing the nipple with his tongue while his hand never stopped its rhythm below, a symphony of touch designed to shatter her composure.

She arched into him, drenched in want, her body a taut bow string of desire. Marcus kissed down her stomach, slow as silk, a trail of fire, until he reached her waistline. He didn't pause. He buried his tongue deep inside her, devouring her like a man starving, consuming her pleasure. Her cries echoed through the walls, a raw, uninhibited sound, as her legs trembled around his head. And when she came, her entire body seized, clawing the sheets, calling his name like it meant salvation, like he was the center of her world. Then he rose, his movements fluid, controlled, betraying no haste.

Pulled down his boxers.

Her eyes widened, a flicker of raw, unrestrained desire in their depths. "...Oh my God," she whispered, her voice breathless, reaching for him, fingers trembling with anticipation. He slid inside her slowly, deliberately, and her nails raked across his back, a silent testament to the intensity. "Don't stop," she begged, breathless, pulling him closer. "Please... Marcus... Don't ever stop."

He moved with purpose slow, deep, deliberate gripping her hips, watching her eyes roll back as their bodies locked into a primal rhythm. Her legs wrapped around him, pulling him in closer, desperate for more. They climaxed together her screams echoing, his silent, internal release, a grim satisfaction that had little to do with pleasure.

Afterward, she lay draped across his chest, her body still twitching in the blissful aftershock, utterly spent, completely trusting. He held her gently. Kissed her forehead. His touch tender, belying the cold calculation in his mind. But his eyes…

They were fixed on the ceiling, unseeing, reflecting only the distant city lights. Calculating. Already planning the next move. His burner phone, kept hidden beneath his pillow, buzzed on the nightstand, a silent, urgent summons from Damon. A single text: "Be ready in 20. -D"

He rose gently, careful not to disturb her, kissed her again, then dressed in silence, his movements efficient, practiced. She stirred, blinking up at him through heavy-lidded eyes. "Everything okay?" she mumbled, her voice thick with sleep and contentment. He nodded, already halfway out the door. "Just something I gotta handle.

A meeting."She smiled sleepily, completely unaware of the true nature of his world, of the intricate web of lies he wove around them both. "You always look serious when you say that."He didn't reply. He couldn't. The truth would shatter her.

A Silent Throne

Twenty minutes later, Marcus stood outside in the chill night air as Damon's blacked-out Maybach rolled to the curb like a presidential motorcade, its engine a barely audible hum. The back door swung open with hydraulic grace. No words exchanged, only a silent acknowledgement. Marcus slid in.

Damon didn't greet him. He was dressed in a dark wool overcoat, gloves on, jaw clenched, a man on the edge of a precipice. The air inside smelled of sandalwood, expensive leather, and unspoken dominance. They rode in silence, the car a bubble of power cutting through the sleeping city.

The car took them south, away from the grimy corners and neon-lit storefronts of Damon's visible empire, toward Baltimore's glittering waterfront district—a place of glass towers, private security, and whispers behind silk curtains, where the real power resided. When they arrived, a valet in a tailored vest opened the door with practiced deference. Damon and Marcus ascended a private elevator, its interior lined in rich mahogany and polished gold, an ascent into the upper echelons of influence.

The doors opened directly into a penthouse suite, vast and opulent, bathed in soft amber light. A fully stocked bar glowed in the corner, reflecting the city lights. Thick cigar smoke drifted toward the ceiling like a slow-moving storm, a haze of power and unspoken deals. The floor-to-ceiling view overlooked the Inner Harbor, glittering with cold reflections, a cityscape laid bare beneath their feet.

Inside the room sat power. Not street power, but institutional power. A congressman from the 7th District, his face etched with weary ambition. A developer with ties to federal transportation contracts, his hands deep in the city's infrastructure. An archbishop whose ring had kissed more cheeks than any elected official in the city, his influence reaching into every home.

And a judge retired, but still very much in play, his past rulings a tapestry of influence. They spoke in half-truths, in coded language, in promises of "urban renewal" that masked massive profits, of backroom deals cemented by quiet favors.

Marcus didn't sit.

He stood in the corner silent, still, eyes flicking from face to face, absorbing every gesture, every nuance, every unspoken agreement. He didn't belong to their world yet. Not officially. But he would. He was studying them, learning their language.

He studied how Damon spoke casually yet calculated, every word chosen for maximum impact. He saw how Damon placed pressure without raising his voice, how he traded future silence for present action, how he held them all in a delicate balance. Every move Damon made was chess. Marcus was already memorizing the board, anticipating the next several moves.

Later, in the elevator, the silence thick with the scent of power, Damon finally spoke. "You see how they look at me?" he asked, his voice low, a conspiratorial murmur. Marcus nodded. They looked at Damon with a mixture of respect, fear, and reluctant admiration. "They don't fear me because I'm dangerous, Marcus. Not just that. They fear me because I know things they don't want said. Things that could unravel their entire lives."

He turned, his gaze sharp, penetrating. "That's power, Marcus. Real power isn't pulling a trigger. It's pulling strings. It's knowing who owes whom, what secrets lie buried, and when to use them." Marcus looked out at the city lights receding beneath them. His jaw flexed. He was learning. And he was hungry. For that kind of power.

The Setup: Reggie's Fall

By now, Reggie's plan had grown roots, like a parasitic vine choking Damon's carefully cultivated network. He had quietly built a crew of his own fractured pieces of Damon's empire bonded together by greed and short-sighted loyalty. He operated just under the surface, careful not to stir up noise in neighborhoods where money still needed to move, where Damon's gaze was constant.

Damon didn't rush to act. He let Reggie feel invincible, let him expand, let him believe he was outsmarting his mentor. He allowed the illusion of success to bloom, only to wither it.Then, all at once, everything collapsed. A silent, coordinated strike.

Three crew outposts were hit simultaneously not with bullets and flashy sirens, but with surgical efficiency, like a master surgeon excising a tumor.

- One stash spot was raided by Damon's black-ops team disguised in stolen tactical gear, clearing out millions in product and cash without a single gunshot.

- A local bar acting as a key drop site was emptied during off-hours, its contents vanished, its security cameras mysteriously blank.

- Four key lieutenants from Reggie's new crew were snatched up in black vans at traffic lights, disappearing into the night without a trace. Quiet. Clean. Undetected.

No gunshots. No chaos. No headlines. Dead bodies bring cops. Headlines bring scrutiny. Whispers, and silent disappearances, built empires. Reggie never saw it coming. The carefully laid trap had sprung shut.

The Meeting

Reggie got the call like it was any other night, a routine summons. "Spot's changing," Damon said over the phone, his voice calm, even friendly. "Too many ears around the regular place. Cops feel close. We need to talk somewhere quieter. Meet me at the old docks, warehouse 17."

Reggie didn't question it. He'd known Damon too long, trusted him, believed he was indispensable. He rolled through the docks in his matte-black Charger, the harbor air heavy with salt and fog, the scent of decay masking the scent of betrayal. He even left his Glock in the stash spot under the driver's seat a sign of comfort, of history, of how much he fatally underestimated the moment.

He found Damon standing under a single, buzzing halogen lamp near the edge of an unfinished warehouse. The bulb flickered overhead, casting long, shifting shadows, like it could sense what was about to happen. "Yo, D," Reggie said, stepping out of the car, a wary smile on his face. "Damn, this place is mad quiet. You sure about this? Feels a little… isolated." Damon said nothing. He simply lit a cigar, the flare of the match briefly illuminating his impassive face. Took a slow pull, the scent of expensive tobacco filling the damp air.

"You remember what I taught you, Reggie?" Damon asked, his voice calm, dangerously even. Reggie tilted his head, confused. "Huh? Taught me what, bro?" "About loyalty. About structure. About the cost of betrayal." Reggie's grin faltered, a cold dread seeping into him. "Of course, bro. I'm here, ain't I? Always loyal." He started to reach for his hip, a sudden, desperate instinct.

From the deeper shadows behind Damon, figures stepped forward three of Damon's most trusted men, all in black, faces blank, moving with silent, predatory grace. They were Damon's enforcers, his silent assassins. Reggie turned, a forced, half-joking laugh escaping him. "Yo, what's this? Some kind of joke, D?" One of them struck.

A pipe, swung with brutal precision, connected with the back of Reggie's knees. Reggie crumpled, a strangled groan escaping him, his legs giving out. Before he could scream, before he could utter another sound, a burlap sack was pulled roughly over his head, plunging him into darkness. They dragged him into the warehouse.

The Lesson

Inside, it smelled of rust, salt, and blood already spilled a scent that clung to the air like a premonition. They tied him to a metal chair, arms secured tightly with reinforced wire, his struggles futile. Damon stood ten feet away, still smoking his cigar, eyes unreadable, a silent judge.

Marcus watched from the deepest shadows behind a support beam silent, still, his breath steady, his hands in his coat pockets. His expression was impassive, absorbing the brutal lesson with clinical detachment. Reggie's screams echoed, raw and desperate, as the tools came out: pliers, wires, a blowtorch that hissed like a viper, its flame a cruel beacon in the dim light. They didn't ask questions. They didn't make threats. They taught. A brutal, agonizing lesson in consequence.

Each scream was punctuation to Damon's silent decree. Each crack of bone was a reminder of the unforgiving laws of the empire. Finally, when Reggie was little more than a broken, whimpering mass, Damon stepped forward, his voice cutting through the bloodied silence.

WHISPERS IN THE WIRE

"You failed me, Reggie. You didn't just break a rule. You cracked the spine of the system we built. You thought I wouldn't see it? That you could build your pathetic little kingdom on my foundation?" Reggie, broken and blood-soaked, sobbed into the gag, his body trembling uncontrollably. "You remember what I taught you?" Damon asked again, crouching beside him, his voice soft, almost paternal, a chilling contrast to the scene. Reggie couldn't answer.

Didn't need to. "Order. Loyalty. Legacy," Damon recited, the words a chilling mantra. He stood. Nodded to his men, a single, definitive gesture. One clean shot to the head. A merciful end to the agonizing lesson.

Then silence. Absolute. Final.

Aftermath

Outside, the harbor wind had grown cold, carrying the damp scent of the bay.Damon stepped into the darkness beside Marcus, his silhouette merging with the deeper shadows."You learn something tonight?" Damon asked, his voice low, assessing.

Marcus nodded, eyes locked on the trail of blood that had reached the warehouse door, a dark stain against the concrete."Yes," he said. The lesson was clear: absolute control, absolute consequence.Damon turned, took one long drag from his cigar, and flicked the glowing end into the darkness, a single ember arching into the night like a falling star. "Good," he said. "Then we're just getting started."

Chapter Six

The Long Game

Senior year arrived like a curtain call, the final act of Marcus Caldwell's carefully constructed performance. He had made it through the gauntlet with his mask firmly intact top of his class, captain of the basketball team, early acceptance to three Ivy League schools, a portfolio of community service projects that gleamed like polished brass, and a reputation so clean it glowed.

In the yearbook, they called him "Most Likely to Lead the Revolution." But no one knew he already had. He had worn the mask well. It had become a second skin, indistinguishable from his own flesh. he scholar. The attentive boyfriend. The model student. The cold, precise operator. Every polite smile he offered, every easy laugh shared in the lunchroom, every highlight reel dunk that brought the Worthington crowd to its feet,it all served one quiet, singular purpose: vengeance. His world had become a chessboard, every interaction a move, every relationship a piece to be deployed. And he had turned his entire life into a controlled illusion, a masterpiece of misdirection. But illusions require precision. And precision was Marcus's religion.

Karen: The Line He Couldn't Untangle

Karen was all-in. More than a pawn now, she had become his solace, his comfort, the only person who made him almost forget the crushing weight of what he carried. Almost. There were moments, brief and fleeting, when he allowed himself to sink into the warmth of her presence, to imagine a different life.

She made plans with hope in her eyes, soft laughter in her throat, her dreams intertwined with his, utterly trusting. She spoke of shared apartments in distant cities, whispered dreams of a future together into his chest at night, her breath soft against his skin. "Where do you see us in five years, Marcus?" she asked one night, curled beneath his arm, her voice laced with innocent anticipation.

Marcus stared at the ceiling, his mind miles away, a ghost in their intimate moment. "Somewhere far away," he murmured, the words true but incomplete. "Clean slate. A fresh start." "Together?" she pressed, her voice soft. He smiled faintly, a practiced curve of his lips. Kissed her forehead. "Always."

But in the pit of his soul, cold and unyielding, he knew the truth: Her father had killed his. And love, however real in fleeting moments, could never outrun that kind of blood. Not for him. Not for a man whose very purpose was built on that foundation of betrayal.

The Perfect Illusion

Marcus had Harold Grayford under comprehensive surveillance:

- Laptop mirrored, every keystroke, every file copied.

- Phone cloned, every call, every text, every location tracked.

- Cameras outside his house tapped, a constant stream of visuals.

- Financials monitored, every illicit transaction flagged.

- Private folders decrypted, exposing a web of corruption.

He had built a dossier so thick it could blackmail a mayor and bury a career, a meticulous, undeniable record of Grayford's transgressions.But Marcus waited. The takedown had to be surgical, not emotional. It couldn't be traced back to him. It had to be a detonation with no visible fuse.

Then, one night, while scanning Harold's encrypted files, Marcus found something chilling: A message. A folder. A name. "Stryker." Reggie. Marcus's breath stilled. The folder held audio logs and messages revealing that Reggie had been feeding Harold classified intel, locations, low-level aliases, movement details, all in hopes of helping law enforcement dismantle Damon's massive empire. It was betrayal layered on betrayal, a viper eating its own tail.And it was about to be used against them both, a weapon that would sever the last remaining ties to his past.

Reggie was already dead. But no one knew that, except Marcus and Damon. And now, the rest of the world would find out in a way neither of them could have predicted.

A Death Rewritten

Marcus got to work. His hands flew across the keyboard, a furious ballet of keystrokes. He took the real footage from the night Reggie died, low lighting, grainy security angles, silhouettes under a single, flickering halogen lamp. The brutal, undeniable truth. Then he replaced one figure in the video with a deepfake, an eerily perfect, digitally rendered Harold Grayford.

The deepfake was clean, eerily natural. From the stance to the flick of the cigar, the lighting matched perfectly, and the motion flowed without a glitch. The audio was rebuilt from voice samples harvested from Harold's own surveillance, spliced and manipulated to fit the new narrative. Layered in, stitched seamlessly with Reggie's final, muffled screams, it painted a masterpiece of murder, Harold Grayford, caught red-handed, executing a known criminal.

By the time he finished, the world would believe Harold Grayford had executed Reggie in cold blood, a rogue cop turned murderer. And Reggie? He vanished without a trace, his body disposed of by Damon's men. Nobody. No witness. Just a story told through manipulated pixels and perfect timing, a story that would consume Harold's whole world.

Before the Ceremony

Graduation day dawned bright, cloudless, still. A deceptive calm before the storm. Outside the auditorium, families mingled in small, excited clusters, their faces bright with pride and anticipation. Marcus stood with Veronica, the quiet tension in her face broken only by a radiant, almost fragile pride.

She smoothed the front of his gown with shaking hands, her eyes glistening. "You look like your father," she said, tears forming, a catch in her voice. "Except maybe a little more serious. He always had that smirk." "Gotta keep the tradition alive," Marcus said with a small, uncharacteristic smirk of his own, a ghost of his old self. Just then, Drew approached, dressed in a dark gray suit, sunglasses hanging from his collar, his expression a mix of awe and lingering sorrow. He hugged Veronica tightly, then turned to Marcus, his eyes searching. "I can't lie, son," Drew said, his voice rough. "I didn't think you'd make it through all this... not without losing yourself completely. This darkness." Marcus held his gaze, an unspoken understanding passing between them. "Maybe I did, Drew. Maybe I just learned to live with the loss. To carry it."

Drew's expression tightened, a flicker of pain, but he nodded. "Your father would've been damn proud today. Not just the grades, not the fancy school... proud of the strength. The discipline. The man you've become." "Thanks, Drew," Marcus said quietly, the words the closest he could come to expressing gratitude. Drew pulled him into a brief, strong hug, then stepped back. Veronica smiled through her tears, her heart full. "Go make your walk, baby. Go get what you earned."

The Walk

They filed into the slow, majestic roll of *Pomp and Circumstance*, students arranged alphabetically by name, their graduation robes flaring behind them like new wings.

The air in the auditorium was thick with anticipation, the hum of hundreds of expectant voices.

Marcus took his seat beside Karen, the stiff fabric of their gowns rustling. She squeezed his hand, beaming, her face alight with innocent joy. "Can you believe this?" she whispered, her voice bubbling with excitement. "We actually made it." Marcus looked around, the teeming crowd, the proud faculty, the distant press cameras poised to capture every triumphant moment. He saw Harold Grayford in the stands, a proud father, oblivious. "I can," he said, his voice low, almost a murmur.

Because he'd imagined this day since the first shot rang out at Liberty Heights, since the blood stained the Edgewood pavement. But not for celebration. For retribution. For the unleashing. Names were called. Applause rose in waves. Flashbulbs popped, brief, blinding bursts of light. And then "Marcus Elijah Caldwell."

He rose, walked with purpose, his movements fluid, unhurried, a man moving toward destiny. He shook the principal's hand, took his diploma, and looked directly into the crowd, where the world was about to shift on its axis, irrevocably.

Diploma in hand, he stood beside Karen and the others, smiling for the pictures. Talking. Laughing. Perfectly normal. The golden boy. Then it happened.

The Release

Across the city, emails launched from untraceable servers, a silent, digital explosion.

- Anonymous messages to Internal Affairs, pinpointing the precise files, the exact time codes.

- Secure dumps to local and national journalists, major news desks receiving packages of encrypted data.

- A drive sent via anonymous courier to a prominent civil rights attorney with deep contacts in the press, guaranteeing maximum exposure and legal leverage.

The files included:

- The meticulously crafted deepfake video footage of Harold Grayford executing Reggie Sykes, a grim, undeniable recording.

- Metadata tying Harold to internal cover-ups, showing his hand in obscuring evidence and manipulating official reports.

- Financial transactions suggesting illicit payments, a shadowy trail of bribes and kickbacks that led back to Grayford.

- And whispers, just whispers, enough to plant the seed, of a "criminal consortium" possibly tied to Damon Hughes, creating a plausible scapegoat, drawing attention away from Marcus.

The leak wasn't fire. It was fog, dense, disorienting, and impossible to ignore. It choked the city, blinding the very systems it sought to expose. Karen's phone buzzed. Then her friends'. Then a teacher's, their faces paling, expressions twisting from joy to shock. Murmurs turned to gasps, then to horrified shouts as news spread through the auditorium like wildfire.

At the edge of the parking lot, police sirens approached, not celebratory, but urgent, piercing. Two cruisers stopped, lights flashing. Officers stepped out, grim-faced, moving with purpose.

Harold Grayford was arrested on-site, in his pressed suit, among the proud parents and cheering graduates. Stunned. Confused. Disarmed. His face, once proud, now etched with disbelief, then dawning horror. People recorded it on their phones. Journalists swarmed, their cameras flashing, microphones thrust forward. Some screamed in outrage. Others stood in silent awe, witnessing a public execution of reputation. Marcus never looked directly at the scene.

He kept his back turned. Spoke casually to a teacher. Laughed politely at something Karen, now pale and trembling, whispered to him, her eyes wide with terror and confusion. But he heard it all. Every siren. Every shout. Every click of the handcuffs. And he knew this was his moment. This was the first wave of the tsunami.

Epilogue of a Victory

Later that night, alone in his room, the house quiet, Marcus sat in the dark. His cap and gown lay draped over

72

his desk, a discarded costume. Screens glowed with endless coverage:

"Local Cop Arrested in Shocking Video Tie to Disappearance of Former Gang Lieutenant. City Rocked by Corruption Scandal."

Damon's name wasn't mentioned in the official reports. Only rumors, vague suggestions, enough to cast a shadow without concrete proof. The system had been cracked, not broken, not shattered beyond repair, but bent. Exposed. The cracks were visible now. And Marcus Caldwell? Still in the fog. Still a ghost. Unseen. Unnamed. Untouched. The boy who lost his father had become something more. Something infinitely more dangerous. A quiet storm. A force of reckoning. And the war...

was far from over. It had just begun.

Chapter Seven

The Reconstruction

The city was still reeling from the fallout. Harold Grayford was on every news channel, his image grainy and frozen in that damning deepfake, a bullet fired in digital silence, his reputation now bleeding out in real time. The formal charges were mounting, a slow, methodical dismantling of his life. Reggie remained a ghost, presumed dead, whispered about in police backchannels and barbershop corners, a cautionary tale.

But Marcus Caldwell?

He walked the streets like mist, present but never visible, a phantom of consequence. Powerful, but never loud, his influence a silent ripple in the city's undercurrents.

The takedown had happened. The first target had fallen.

But it wasn't the end. It was just the blueprint, the proof of concept. The beginning of a much larger, darker ambition.

The Choice

He had offers. Full rides from Yale, Columbia, Princeton. Ivy League doors opened wide with gold trim, beckoning him towards a conventional, brilliant future. They wanted Marcus for his intellect, his incredible story of overcoming adversity, his polished smile. The boy who had pulled himself up by his bootstraps.

But he said no. Politely. Firmly.

Because college wasn't where wars were won. Not the war he was fighting. It was too slow, too public, too constrained. One evening, Marcus sat across from Damon in the war room, the harbor lights behind them twinkling like static, reflecting in the polished surface of the table. A tension, unspoken but palpable, hung between them. "You're serious?" Damon asked, swirling bourbon in a heavy crystal glass, his eyes narrowed, studying Marcus as if he were a new, unpredictable variable. "You're walking away from the Ivy Leagues?

From a future that most kids would kill for, for basic training?" Marcus nodded, his gaze steady, unyielding. "I'm not doing this for degrees, Damon. I need something different. Something sharper." Damon studied him, silent, a slow comprehension dawning in his eyes. "You're playing the long game. Even longer than I thought." "I need to disappear for a while.

Learn what I don't know. Build relationships with people who operate on a different plane. Learn discipline from a different angle. Get inside the system. The real system. Not just the cops on the street, but the military-industrial complex. The global apparatus." "You think the military gives you that access?" Damon mused, taking a sip of his bourbon. "That kind of... transformative power?" "I don't want access," Marcus said, his voice hardening, revealing the deeper truth of his ambition. "I want transformation.

I want to become a weapon so precise, so untraceable, they'll never see me coming. I want to understand how they train their elite. How they break men down and build them back stronger. How they control and deploy force on a global scale." Damon finally nodded, a flicker of admiration in his eyes. "Special Forces?" "That's the goal. The pinnacle." Damon leaned back, a faint smile playing on his lips, a mixture of pride and a chilling understanding. "You'll see shit out there that changes you, Marcus. Things you can't unsee. Things that will make everything you've done so far feel small." Marcus didn't flinch. His eyes were cold, resolute. "I already have. And it's only made me hungrier."

The Goodbye

Karen met him at the lake, the very spot where they'd first talked about poetry, the future, and everything they thought love could outrun. The air was soft, a gentle breeze rustling the leaves, a cruel contrast to the storm brewing between them.

She wore a simple summer dress, her eyes puffy like she hadn't slept, her face etched with a desperate confusion. "I don't understand, Marcus," she whispered, her voice trembling. "You said you got into Columbia. I saw the letter. We had plans." "I turned it down." "Why?" The single word was a plea, an accusation.

"Because that's not my path, Karen. Not anymore. Maybe it never was." She stepped closer, her hands reaching for his, desperate for connection. "Then what is? What is more important than us?" "I enlisted," he said flatly, the words like stones dropping into still water. "Army. I leave for basic in three weeks. Maybe longer if I make it to Special Forces training."

Her breath caught, a strangled sound. "No," she whispered, tears already welling in her eyes, blurring the perfect image of him. "Marcus, no. You don't have to do this. Your father would want you to live a life, to be safe." "I do," he said, his voice quiet, final, unyielding. "This is bigger than me. Bigger than us. It's a debt I have to pay, a war I have to fight. And I can't do it here. Not like this."

Karen's hands trembled as she reached for his, clutching them desperately. "Then let me wait for you. However long it takes. I'll be here when you come back. We can make this work." He squeezed her hand once, a last, fleeting connection, then gently, deliberately, let go. His touch was firm, but his release was absolute.

"No," he said, his voice quiet but final, carrying the weight of an unspoken pain. "You can't wait for someone who doesn't know if he's coming back. And you can't wait for someone who isn't coming back the same. I'm already gone, Karen. The boy you knew... he's already gone."

Tears streamed down her cheeks, silent rivers of heartbreak. "I love you, Marcus," she choked out, her voice raw with agony. He looked away, his gaze distant, fixed on the shimmering surface of the lake, refusing to meet her heartbroken eyes. He couldn't. It would shatter the last fragments of his resolve. "That's why I'm letting you go." He left her standing there, silhouetted by the dying sunset, a figure of profound sorrow, shattered but, in time, perhaps whole again.And he didn't look back. He couldn't afford to.

The Shadow Society

While his classmates planned parties, internships, and dorm move-ins, embarking on lives of privilege and expectation, Marcus disappeared deeper into the underworld but not as a criminal. As a curator. An architect. A silent, guiding hand.

He worked with Damon, meeting in secure, untraceable locations, to begin shifting the very foundation of their empire, one layer at a time. No more dope runs. No more petty turf wars. Those were noisy, old-world tactics. Obsolete. The new game was silence. Information. Influence. Precision. Leverage.

He used the network Damon had built, the hackers, the crooked accountants, the government insiders, the street-level informants, and began filtering them. Refining them. Who believed in something bigger than money? Who had a conscience, however buried? Who could be repurposed for a grander mission? Who could be trusted with a truth that would unravel the powerful?

And slowly, under cover of coded messages, encrypted communications, and closed, unmonitored doors, he began constructing a different kind of organization. A society. Not a gang. Not a government agency. A ghost force. A silent hand of justice operating outside the law. They didn't wear uniforms. They didn't share names, operating under aliases, their true identities shielded even from each other.

But they moved in the dark, documenting corruption, leaking evidence with devastating timing, ruining careers with one well-timed upload, one anonymous tip. Corrupt cops. Venal judges. Compromised politicians. Corporate criminals.

No one was above scrutiny.

No one was untouchable.

Each member of the network was anonymous, even to each other, a truly decentralized, unbreakable web. They didn't chase headlines, evading the limelight. They chased accountability, truth, and a quiet, brutal justice. Their only rule: stay in the dark. Be unseen. It was the only place truth could survive, the only place justice could be truly served.

The Departure

Marcus left the city quietly. No party. No grand send-off. No tearful goodbyes beyond Karen's. Just a firm handshake from Damon at the desolate train station, the roar of an approaching locomotive filling the air, and a shared silence that said more than words ever could. It was an acknowledgment of their bond, of the unspoken understanding between them.

"You're becoming more than I ever imagined, Marcus," Damon said, looking out over the tracks, his face unreadable. "A force of nature." "I'm just becoming who I need to be, Damon. Who I was forged to be." "Keep your edge," Damon warned, his voice low, a final piece of advice. "Out there, in the Army, they'll try to dull it. To make you part of their machine. Don't let them."

Marcus gave a small, chilling smile, a shadow of the boy he once was. "They won't succeed. I'm not joining their machine, Damon. I'm learning how to dismantle it." As the train pulled in, its massive bulk hissing steam, Marcus stepped on, his duffel over his shoulder. He moved with a quiet purpose, a man embarking on a pilgrimage, not a journey. He didn't wave goodbye.

He just disappeared into the crowd, a shadow swallowed by the vast, indifferent maw of the military. A new chapter, darker and more complex, was about to begin. The seeds of vengeance had been sown, nurtured, and now, they were about to be transplanted into the harsh, unforgiving soil of global warfare.

www.ingramcontent.com/pod-product-compliance
Lightning Source LLC
Chambersburg PA
CBHW060651260626
47161CB00008B/3094